THE SECRET LIFE OF
JAMIE B

Ceri Worman

ORCHARD BOOKS

Contents

CHAPTER 1

Shot by a Stun Gun

Hi – the name's B., Jamie B. International Secret Agent, licensed to thrill. If you want to know how to become a superspy then listen up! I'm going to tell you all about my new mission. There'll be action, danger, and love interest too... The question is, can you stand the pace?

A secret agent like me has only two basic states – asleep or alert. This morning I'm on *red* alert:

Jamie B. dives out of bed, checks his slippers for scorpions, then commando-rolls across the hall to avoid enemy sensors. In the bathroom, he whips back the shower curtain - *FAST!* but not fast enough. A robotic hit-man is already lunging towards him.

Metal Man's claws grab Jamie's throat in a grip of steel.

Is this the end for our hero?

With a supreme effort Jamie B. reaches across the sink for his supersonic soap bar and squeezes...

ZZZZaaPPP!

Burning acid bubbles explode over Metal Man. He staggers back clawing madly at his own throat.

Pop! Pop! Pop!

Each bursting bubble leaves a smoking hole of burning steel. Metal Man is dissolving faster than cyanide in champagne.

'I do hope you enjoyed your bubble bath,' says Jamie B.

Metal Man does not reply. He just disappears down the plughole in a slither of silvery slime.

Superspy B. sniffs at the soap bar. It's the first time he's tried this new gadget. **Mmmmm!** He'll be happy to report back to HQ that it's not only lethal, but lemony fresh too.

*

'Jamie, hurry up in the shower, will you! It's the same every morning. What takes you so long?'

That's M.'s voice. She's the boss – at least she thinks she is. I like to play along with her little fantasy. But she has reminded me, Jamie B. is due to report downstairs for orders at 08.00 hours.

I head to my room and check the wardrobe for bugs (real and electrical). All clear.

Now, what to wear? No expensive Italian silk shirt for this mission; I pull on an old T-shirt, jeans and trainers. Once again Jamie B., Superspy and Ladykiller Extraordinaire, is working undercover.

OK, OK. So a summer holiday job washing cars at *Albert's Autos* might not sound as dangerous as tracking nuclear subs in the South Pacific, but orders are orders. Besides, the extra cash helps cover a twelve-year-old's expense account!

M. serves me with a delicious breakfast of golden brown toast and fresh orange juice (shaken, not stirred). She briefs me on the day ahead.

'It's half eight already, Jamie! Hurry up, or you'll miss the bus.'

I twiddle my belt buckle and switch on the decoder:

'The garage is run by a Mr Albert X (surname unknown): white, male, early 50s. Watch his movements carefully and report back at 16.00 hours.'

I switch off the decoder. M. is reaching for the car keys. She sighs, 'I might as well take you myself. Just this once.'

Jamie B. raises an eyebrow. Women – where would we be without them?

I step out of my chauffeur-driven limousine and walk coolly up to a building marked *Albert's Autos – Garage and Shop*. Opening the door I freeze as if shot by a stun gun.

Cue saxophone music. Sitting behind the counter is the best looking female love interest I've ever seen. It's a pity she might get killed before the end of the mission.

She's got dark red hair pulled back into a

smooth pony tail and she's wearing black trousers and a slinky black top. She's superstar beautiful. I raise an eyebrow to express *mild* interest.

Her eyes are green and hypnotic. 'Yes?'

'Yes.' I repeat. 'Oh, yes.'

Her eyes narrow.

'Um…s-s-summer holiday job. Is Albert around?'

She opens her perfect pink lips and shrieks 'DAD!' in a voice that could shatter glass at twenty paces. Might come in handy if we're ever tied up together behind a two-way mirror.

Suddenly a shadow crosses my path. I look up…and up…and up some more. Her dad is as tall as…well, a *very* tall person.

He's wide too. I'd never be able to use my superspy stranglehold technique on *that* tree-trunk neck, even if the future of the world was at risk.

He gives me a pen and a piece of paper. Does he want my autograph? Has the secret identity of Jamie B., Superspy, been rumbled already?

'Name and address, lad,' he says instead, stabbing at the paper with his stubby finger. 'As I said before, we could do wi' someone to wash down the cars and 'elp out. Got any previous?'

'Aye,' I say, slipping smoothly into a blokey, Northern accent. Languages are my speciality. 'Always wash me old ma's car of a Sunday.'

He gives me a strange look but the girl (Kitty I'll call her, because she reminds me of a cat) pounces.

'Don't worry, Dad. He goes to our school. He's a few years below me but I've seen him about.'

Do I? Am I? Why haven't I seen her before? I have been pretty busy with weapon and fitness training lately, and my Babe Alert radar must be on the blink too.

'Right, come wi' me.'

Then it hits me like a fist in the face. I'm starting work now. Real work. Jamie B. washing cars in *Albert's Autos*. It's not really my style. I prefer helicopters, car chases and evil criminals. All that must be to come...

CHAPTER 2

Captain of the Bumsniffers

Albert definitely seems evil to me. He's big and bossy and he's offered to pay me next to nothing.

I decide to code-name him Mr Dad for the purposes of this investigation, because he seems to be the father of the charming and beautiful Kitty. Big Bad Mr Dad with such a gorgeous daughter – how weird is that?

'Car,' says Mr Dad, pointing at one (rather unnecessarily in my opinion).

'Bucket.' He puts it in my hand and water slops onto my jeans. I don't flinch – I'm trained to show no emotion, though perhaps my eyebrow squiggles slightly.

'Cloth,' he adds, putting it into my other hand. 'Know what to do?'

I nod, deciding to follow his policy of using as few words as possible. Perhaps the place is bugged.

'Forty filthy cars.' He spreads his arms wide. 'Clean and shiny by dinnertime. Got that, boy?'

Now Jamie B., International Superspy, isn't used to being called 'boy'. In fact no self-respecting secret agent would let that go.

'Hold it right there, Mr Dad,' says Jamie B. coldly. 'The name's B., Jamie B. Not *"boy"*. It shouldn't take too much brain strain to get that right.'

Mr Dad gives an evil laugh. 'And you can call me Sir, got that - *boy*?' He pushes Jamie B. hard in the chest and pins him against a car.

'And if you stand in the way of my plans to take over the world, you won't even 'ave a brain. Got that too - *boy*?'

'I should warn you, Mr Dad, that I am a black belt in karate. I do not wish to hurt you, but may be forced to do so if—'

Mr Dad raises his huge arm like a weapon, but Jamie B. blocks him and grabs Mr Dad's other arm, twisting it behind his back.

Aaaaggh!

Mr Dad tries to writhe free, overbalances and

slams backwards onto the floor.

Whuummp!

The impact knocks him out cold and he lays there like a fat fish on a slab.

'Wakey, wakey, rise and shine,' says Superspy B., refreshing him with a bucket of dirty water.

Slosshhh!

'Now let me help you clean up.' Jamie B. takes out a handy pocket-sized foil pack. 'It says here that this is the ultimate clean-up cloth. It contains a fast-acting truth drug which activates on contact with the skin. Let's put it to the test.'

He wipes Mr Dad's stubbly face.

'Now, Mr Dad, you are seriously evil. True or false?'

'False,' Mr Dad replies, sadly.

'A total idiot?'

'True.'

Jamie B. grins. The truth drug is definitely working and one hundred per cent accurate. He presses the voice recorder button on his wristwatch.

17

'About these plans to take over the world, Mr Dad. You were saying...?'

'I said clean and shiny by dinnertime. Are you listening, boy?' Mr Dad says, loudly.

'Yes, sir, clean and shiny,' I reply, saluting...and splatting myself in the face with the wet cloth.

He looks at me as if I'm an idiot. The undercover trick is working. He'll never suspect a thing.

I dip the cloth into soapy water and begin my new mission.

Two and a half cars later and I'm still waiting for the action. No ambush, bombs or suspicious characters. My hands are all wet and wrinkly and I'm bored.

Hey, look at me – I'm the star of a new B-movie called *Coldfinger*, now playing in an empty cinema near you!

Surely the world of spying is more exciting than this?

Then it happens.

'That's the one,' a loud voice says, breaking the silence. It sounds as confident as a car alarm and just as annoying. 'I'll take it.'

'What, just like that?' another voice asks. It's Kitty. She's toned down her glass-shattering shriek to a silky purr.

I look up from the car I'm washing and see her standing with the captain of the school rugby team. They are both slavering over the shiniest, sleekest, silveryest, most powerful-looking car I have ever seen.

'Jamie, can you wash this car for our customer,' asks Kitty in a voice that clicks its fingers at me. I pretend not to hear.

'JAMIE!' she shrieks, shattering the wing mirror on a nearby car. 'Do you know who this is?'

I shake my head. "Give me a clue.'

'What?! Think *rugby*.'

'*Hmmm*, you mean that game where grown men huddle together with their faces pressed up against each others'—'

'*This* is Stirling Leech, of course!' she interrupts quickly. 'Captain of the—'

'Bumsniffers?' I say, helpfully.

The sniffer in question chooses to ignore me, but I see a nerve twitch in his rock-hard jaw.

'It's my eighteenth on Saturday, Kitty,' he smarms (so I'm not the only one who thinks she's catty!). 'Sort me out a test drive and you might be in for a ride on Saturday night.'

'Jamie, wash the car while I go through the paperwork with Mr Leech,' Kitty snaps.

She tosses the car keys into my hand. Big mistake.

CHAPTER 3

Poisonous Spider

The keys are in the ignition, the soft top is down, the radio is on louder than loud and Jamie B. is steering around the rocky bends of a winding cliff-top road with the evil villain, Mr Dad, hot on his tail.

Suddenly, Mr Dad's jet-black Lotus Esprit screeches up to Jamie B.'s side, trying to force him over the edge.

Bash. Bash. BASH!

Oh no! Jamie B. can hear Mr Dad's evil laugh ringing in his ears as his car lurches drunkenly and he loses control. The car tips up, tumbling over and over in sinister slow-motion cartwheels down the cliff side.

Is this the end for our hero?

Just in time, Superspy B. presses the eject button and hurtles into the air. His parachute opens and he looks down to see his sleek,

silvery car slam into a tree and burst
into flames.

BOOM!

On the cliff top Mr Dad is laughing so much he
doesn't even see Jamie B. floating gently in the
air above him as he pulls away. Nor does he see
Jamie B. take out a hand-held remote control
and fire a magnetic locking device onto the
roof of Mr Dad's car below.

Now Jamie B. is driving Mr Dad's car for him.
It's the biggest toy he's ever had and he's
having fun! Jamie B. accelerates the Lotus,
hard and fast.

'Stop!' cries Mr Dad, slamming on the brakes
and hauling on the steering wheel. He
knows that missing the next bend means
certain death - if the fall doesn't kill him, the
bay full of man-eating sharks will.

The car speeds straight ahead, crashing into
the safety barrier.

'Nooooooo!'

'What are you smirking at? You should be
working.' Kitty's eyes flash in at me. I switch off

the radio and press the button to raise the soft top.

'Just testing the steering,' I say.

She ignores me and turns to Stirling. 'Ready to go then,' she purrs. 'And I'm afraid I'll have to come with you. Rules are rules.'

It is at this point that Jamie B. knows what he has to do. I can't leave her alone with this bumsniffing maniac. Kitty's honour is at stake. Never mind the safety of the motoring public.

I get out of the car but before going back to my bucket I make sure that the back door is left slightly open.

They are so busy fiddling with the radio and testing all the gadgets that they don't even notice me double back. A moment later I crawl into the back of the car and worm my way under a convenient rug on the floor.

'Off we go then, Stirling,' Kitty says. But above the noise of the radio I'm sure I hear him mumble, 'Actually…er…I don't drive.'

I try not to laugh. Can't even drive? Jamie B. could teach him a thing or two…

They open their doors and walk round to

swap seats. I keep still and try to blend into the background which is difficult wrapped in a tartan rug on a black floor.

'If you don't mind me asking, why do you want this car when you can't drive?' I hear Kitty enquire.

'No problemo,' Stirling says, all smarmy again. 'Dad's booked me some lessons. I'll be behind the wheel in a month or two.'

'You're very confident.' Kitty is purring once more as this time she slides into the driver's seat and closes the door.

'Natural talent. I'm good with my hands.'

At this point I see Kitty grasp the handbrake. 'Need any help?' he adds.

'No thanks,' Kitty giggles. Then she starts the engine, releases the brake, moves smoothly into first gear and we're off.

We drive for a few minutes with Kitty doing the sales pitch – 'sunroof', 'power steering', 'climate control' – when a horrific sight catches my eye.

Perched on Kitty's knee, like a big, poisonous spider, is Leech's hairy hand. A finger twitches and it starts to scuttle up her leg. Kitty miaows in surprise and slaps it away – hard.

'In case you hadn't noticed, I'm the one driving and my leg is not a gear stick!' she hisses.

'Hey, calm down. Let's just enjoy the ride,' Leech says. Well *he* certainly is.

Kitty puts her foot down and the car zooms away even faster. It's only when I see his filthy hand poised to strike for a second time that Jamie B. takes action.

I rear up off the floor with the rug still covering me. To the untrained eye I might look like some kind of crazy, tartan ghost, but this is, in fact, a sophisticated anti-sleazeball shock tactic.

Grabbing Leech's clammy fingers I yell, 'Hands off!' at the top of my voice.

And that's when we crash the car.

CHAPTER 4
Slash Victim

Kitty, in a state of shock at the sudden sight of a tartan ghost in her rear-view mirror, slams on the brakes. Then the car behind crashes into the back of us and catapults me headfirst towards the windscreen. Suddenly an airbag inflates and the last thing I remember is bouncing off it...

The next thing I know, Kitty's voice is purring in my ear, 'Don't speak. There's been an accident. You hit your head on the edge of a car seat and blacked out for a while.'

Just like my hero's dry Martini: I am shaken, not stirred. Kitty fills me in on the details, but it's hard to listen because Leech is moaning, 'My car! My car!'

'Oh, shut up, you idiot!' Kitty screeches at him. 'Can't you see this boy's life is in the balance? Head injuries are serious!'

I risk opening my eyes and stare straight into Kitty's concerned face. Her eyes have changed colour. They're now kind of greeny-blue, like a troubled sea – the sort of eyes you might drown in if you're not wearing a life-jacket.

'It's OK, don't worry.' Kitty is stroking my arm and I'm sure I hear that sax music again. 'I've already phoned for a—'

'What the...?' Leech interrupts.

At the same moment we all hear a strange whirring sound, which is getting louder and louder. Leaves and litter are spinning round and round in whirlwinds outside the car. Through the side window I see a helicopter appear in the sky.

So this is it – not a sax solo but a surprise enemy invasion and Jamie B. helpless to defend his country.

'It's an air ambulance!' Leech yells above the racket. 'Why on earth did you—?'

'I didn't!' Kitty shouts back, looking totally mystified.

The helicopter lands on a patch of waste ground nearby and within seconds two men dressed in white are at the car door.

'Air ambulance. You reported a stabbing – lucky we were in the area. Where's the slash victim?'

'Slash victim?' Kitty repeats. 'I phoned to report a crash victim.'

The two men look at each other. 'Told you that radio's no good,' says one.

'Either that or you want to get your ears fixed,' says the other.

'You what?' says the first.

'Pardon?' says the other.

'A-hem – *this* is the victim,' Kitty announces loudly.

Suddenly they're both looking at me lying on the back seat. For some reason I feel like a fraud.

'It's a head injury,' Kitty says gravely. 'And I know they have to be checked. He passed out.'

I close my eyes, as if to demonstrate.

'Uh huh, we'll just wipe off some of this blood and see how bad it is.'

'Blood?' I put my hand to my forehead. It feels sticky. When I look at my fingers they're red. It's not tomato sauce, not raspberry sauce, not red ink, but blood.

REAL BLOOD.
IN GLORIOUS 3-D TECHNICOLOR!
I pass out again.

Jamie B. is in trouble. Glamorous Kitty Galore may have come over to his side and helped him escape Mr Dad's pool of piranhas by hi-jacking a helicopter, but things are not going well. Out of the swirling clouds ahead a red war plane marked DAD 1 is heading straight for them, its guided missiles locked on target.

'We're going to die!' screams Kitty, but even before her words are out Jamie B. has sent the helicopter into a steep dive. His quick reflexes save their lives but their tail takes a direct hit from the missile. The helicopter is spiralling out of control in a plume of black smoke.

'Jump for it!' yells Jamie B. as he wrestles the door open. Air rushes in, knocking them sideways. With almost superhuman strength, he pushes Kitty out and leaps after her.

GERONIMO!

For a few moments Superspy B. is spinning

round and round in space, fighting to stay upright. At last he can see the tiny mapped-out streets below and yanks at his rip-cord.

Nothing happens. The parachute doesn't open.

He pulls again.

Nothing happens.

The earth is hurtling towards him and the wind is roaring in his ears.

Is this the end for our hero?

Suddenly a warm hand grabs his own and a familiar voice whispers—

'Jamie, you're dribbling. Here's a tissue.'

Wow! I think Kitty likes me. Here I am flying in an air ambulance with an oxygen mask strapped to my face and a beautiful girl holding my hand while I drift in and out of consciousness. For a few wild, wonderful minutes I feel on top of the world. But when they wheel me out to the casualty department on a stretcher, I come back down to earth with a bang!

All of a sudden my head starts throbbing like

a nuclear alert button two seconds before meltdown. I feel sick.

'We'll leave you here with your girlfriend,' says one of the medics. 'Good luck, mate.'

I don't even have the energy to wave, or to explain that Kitty – unfortunately – is not my girlfriend. Not yet anyway. She's been speaking to a nurse but now she comes back over to me.

'It'll be about a fifteen-minute wait,' she says, looking concerned. 'Will you be all right? You look very pale.'

She's right. Strangely, I don't feel like an International Superspy any more. I feel just like…an ordinary boy with a head injury. I feel scared and weak and sort of alone, but not quite alone because Kitty's here and I want to thank her but I don't even know her real name.

'What d'they call you?' I mumble.

She smiles. 'If you mean my name, it's Katie. Katie Cat. But they call me Kitty, for obvious reasons. I hate it.'

Of course she does. I try to smile back but my mouth feels out of control, like a mad dentist has just given me a thousand fillings.

'Katie,' I mumble, 'thanks for being here. It means a lot to me.'

And then I lean over and throw up right in her lap.

CHAPTER 5

An Hour to Live

Jamie B. is critically injured and lies hooked up to a life-support machine in hospital.

A hand grips the door handle of the intensive care ward and - ignoring the

PRIVATE KEEP OUT. THIS MEANS YOU!

sign - the tall, bulky figure of Mr Dad walks in.

He strides purposefully across the polished floor and stops at Jamie B.'s bed. He leans over the life support machine looking for the OFF button. His fat finger hovers above the switch. Mr Dad is enjoying the moment - the power of life and death - a view to a kill.

Is this the end for our hero?

As if warned by some basic instinct Jamie B. suddenly kicks out without even the flicker of an eyelid.

HIYAAAH!

There is a satisfying crunch as his foot engages with the enemy—

'Jamie, be careful! You nearly knocked your water jug over – oh thank goodness you're OK!'

Two arms grab me in a bear hug. 'Mum!' I croak, fighting for breath. 'What are you doing here? Where am I?'

'You're lying in a hospital bed after only one day at work. You were fast asleep until your leg went into spasm – oh what am I going to do with you?'

I hug her back, even though this is not Jamie B.'s style. Then, once I have checked that no one is looking, I hug her some more because she feels warm and safe.

That's when I realise that someone important is missing.

'Mum, where's Katie? She was with me until—'

'That girl? She had to go home. She said she had to get cleaned up – she did look a bit of a mess. The doctor told me about the crash, but why you were sitting in the back and without your seat belt on I don't know.'

'What happened to the car?'

'Oh, I think that's been towed back to the garage. Was that girl driving?'

'Katie? Yeah, it was a test run.'

Suddenly M. gets angry and starts talking in capitals. 'REALLY? She doesn't look OLD enough. It's DOWNRIGHT IRRESPONSIBLE letting her drive. I've a good mind to REPORT that garage. Well, that's the end of your work THERE for the summer. You can come and work with ME at the salon when you get better.'

When you get better, M. said, but will I really? I know she's just trying to cheer me up. Such a serious wound must be fatal...

I think of the crowds gathering outside the hospital, the death-bed TV interviews, the radio bulletins and – of course – the special Jamie B. edition of *International Superspy Weekly*, translated into thirty-six languages.

I am not a coward. I can face the worst.

'Mum – the truth. How long have I got?'

She looks at her watch, 'Oh, about an hour I should say.'

An hour? How can she be so calm? Think of all the missions I will never finish, the villains who will walk free, the girls I will never get to—

'The doctor said she'd come and give you a final check-over and then we can go home. Small scalp wound and mild concussion, she said.'

Yeeesssss! Jamie B. is back in action! You only live twice, after all.

M. is talking again. It must be time to switch on the decoder:

'A close call, Jamie B. It seems that Mr Dad is not the only villain on the scene. Keep an eye on Stirling Leech, too – the enemy is everywhere. Go back to Albert's Autos *and work on the girl* (Oh, if you insist!). *She is the key to all this. She seems to be weakening.'*

I switch off the decoder.

'…and clean socks,' M. is saying.

'Mum, give me one more chance at the garage,' I plead, even reaching out to hold her hand. 'I promise not to go on any more test runs – honest.'

'But Jamie…'

'And think how it will be if I walk out of my first job after one day!' I raise an eyebrow. 'I'll be mentally scarred for life – I might never work again.'

That gets her. A superspy must have a way with words as well as weapons. I follow through with a winning Jamie B. smile and another hug. She surrenders. They always do.

'Well, you'll have to stay at home and rest tomorrow. Then we'll see...'

And we all know what that means.

CHAPTER 6
Gruesome Twosome

Jamie B. approaches enemy HQ. *Albert's Autos*. He has decided to confront the villain face to face.

BANG!

Suddenly a bullet whizzes past him and he almost loses an ear. Jamie B. hits the ground fast, rolling over and over to escape the hail of bullets, and dives under a car for cover.

It seems that Mr Dad has prepared a welcoming committee.

Jamie B. props himself up on his elbows and pulls out his mobile phone, aiming it at the roof. 'Don't worry, I've got your number,' he mutters, prodding at the keypad. He brings up a photo image of the sniper and presses 'Call'.

Bleep Bleep Bleeeeeep!

Lethal ultrasonic sonar signals wash over the rooftops, wave after mind-numbing wave.

'Aaaagh!'

The sniper falls from the roof and Jamie B. presses 'End'. 'Nice talking to you,' he says.

He scans the area for more unwelcome surprises and then makes another run for the doors of enemy HQ.

Not a good move. The snipers are everywhere. Two things save his life: his bullet-proof baseball cap and the multiple sonar-sweep mode on his mobile phone. But now he's out of credit...

Slamming the door of the garage shop behind me I find myself gasping for breath and face to face with Mr Dad and Stirling Leech.

They look up from their fiendish plotting and you could cut the atmosphere with a knife. Leech is quick to make the first stab.

'That's the kid – playing silly devils in the back of my Merc. He's the one who distracted Kitty and caused the crash.'

Katie not Kitty, I think to myself, feeling the urge to drive home the point with a superspy karate chop to his chin. But my hands are lethal weapons and I exercise the iron self-control I learned in training.

Mr Dad's bull neck has flushed a dark shade of purple, which matches his nose. I should warn them of my superior fighting strength – it's only fair. But I decide to give them one last chance, I'll try brain power to disarm them first.

'There was a reason why I jumped up in the back seat,' I say slowly and steadily, 'a very good reason.' I raise an eyebrow at Leech who flinches as if he's been shot.

Mr Dad grunts, which I take as a sign of interest.

'Perhaps you would like to explain?' I ask Leech politely.

Leech coughs and starts fiddling with the papers on the counter.

'Ahem. Well, the point is that it happened,' he says crossly. 'What I need to know now, Albert, is if the repairs can be finished before Saturday. There's no time to order a new Merc before the rugby club dance at Swanks.'

Albert's neck has simmered down to a pale lilac.

'Leave it wi' me,' he says. 'Bumper, new wing,

respray. We'll cover the costs, o' course. It'll be in and out of the workshop in a couple of days, right as rain.'

'And driver thrown in as agreed?' Leech asks. 'Where is Kitty by the way?'

'It's 'er morning off.' Albert looks confused. 'Don't know nothing about no driver.'

Leech smiles. Like a shark, he seems to have too many teeth. 'Just call it part of my compensation. She gets to drive me to the rugby club dance and has a free night out as a bonus.'

'Better sort that out with 'er. She's in this afternoon... And what are you still 'ere for?' he suddenly barks at me. 'Blooming holiday work – it's all 'oliday and no work wi' you. This is your last chance. Get those cars washed pronto. Got it?'

I turn to go.

'And one more thing.' Mr Dad's voice is unusually quiet which makes it all the more sinister.

'Yes?'

He comes over to me and I look up...and up...and up into his cold, grey eyes.

'We've got some cars comin' in for repair today. It's a rush job and we've got loyal customers waiting to pay cash in 'and for 'em, so...' He pauses, then suddenly his voice booms, 'DON'T. GO. NEAR. THE. WORKSHOP.' He punctuates each of his words with a jab at my shoulder and by the end of the sentence I'm swaying slightly. 'Repeat.'

'DON'T. GO. NEAR. THE. WORKSHOP,' I parrot, just stopping myself from jabbing him back. Not that I'd reach his shoulder – only his beer-belly.

'Or I'll have your guts for garters,' he adds.

I close the shop door to the sound of vile and villainous laughter from both Mr Dad and Leech – the gruesome twosome.

CHAPTER 7

Following Orders

Of course, DON'T. GO. NEAR. THE. WORKSHOP means YOU. MUST. GO. IN. THE. WORKSHOP when decoded. The question is – how?

I wash cars all morning but my senses are on superspy alert. I try to assess the situation and make a few notes:

1. The workshop is tucked away right behind the main garage and shop area. (See map)

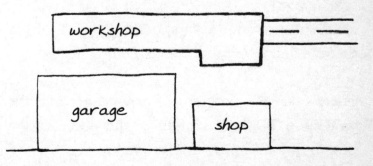

2. There is a separate turn-off from the main road which leads into the mysterious workshop.

3. Two hours ago a transporter arrived with approx. 20 old bangers. They looked ready for the scrap heap.

4. Some of the 'repaired' cars have been loaded back onto the transporter. They look as bad as ever! e.g. battered and scratched, doors which don't match etc.

5. Mr Dad said loyal customers are waiting to pay cash in hand for them. Why?

Conclusion
Something dodgy is going on.
Sounds like a mission for B., Jamie B.!

There's still the problem of how to get into the workshop. If I walk straight up the side road I'm putting myself in the line of enemy fire.

Still puzzling this over, I head into the garage

shop to report that all the cars have been washed. What a surprise to see Katie there! She doesn't look too happy.

Jamie B. gazes into the tearful eyes of his secretary, Miss Katie Spendapenny.

'Oh, Jamie, you were away so long. I thought you were—'

'Not another word, Spendapenny. May I say how wonderful you look this morning.'

She blushes. 'Oh, do you really think so? If only I could be sure there was a certain spy who loved me...?'

'Now you wouldn't want me to give away any top secrets, would you?'

Jamie B. tries to distract her by tossing his hat onto the—

'Careful! You nearly broke the clock!' Katie points to where it's fallen on the floor, along with my baseball cap.

I pick up the clock and hand it back. 'Doesn't time fly?'

She gives me a long look. 'Feeling better now,

then? No sickness or anything?'

My face suddenly feels very hot as I remember the last time I saw her. But superspies don't blush, do they? There must be something wrong with the heating in the shop.

Reaching down for my cap I mumble, 'Look Katie, I'm really sorry about…' Yes, it's definitely the heating, my mouth has dried up too and I can't get the words out.

'Don't worry. Forget it,' she laughs. 'I've got worse things to worry about than vomit on my skirt.'

'What could be worse than that?'

'I've just agreed to drive Stirling Leech to the rugby club dance and be his escort for the evening.'

'Yeah? That really is sick.' At least she's changed her mind about Stirling. It's probably because he's got desert disease – wandering palms.

'Hang on a minute. Why did you agree? You don't have to go.'

'What, after I crashed his car…?'

She doesn't add, *It was all your fault, of*

course! but the thought hangs between us like a poisonous spider ready to strike.

I give up and change the subject fast.

'Anyway, I've washed all the cars now, so I'm waiting for orders.'

'Dad said you can go home – half day.'

This comes as a surprise, especially as he moaned earlier that I never did any work. Does it have anything to do with those old cars coming in for 'repairs'?

'Oh, right, um…can of coke, please. Shaken, not stirred.' I fish around in my pocket for some coins, playing for time because there's still unfinished business to sort out.

'Don't worry about paying. It's on the house.' Her fingers brush mine as she hands me a can. There's that sax music again.

Now she's smiling. 'Well, I'd better sort out this paperwork for those cars. See you tomorrow.'

At this point a thought hits me like a laser shot. Is Katie trying to get rid of me? Is she in on the plot?

'Um, just need the…er… Where…?' And now I'm not playing for time. I'm hopping from foot to foot. Even international superspies are human.

'You mean the little boys' room?' She's laughing but I can't see the joke.

'I most certainly do not! I mean the...*big* boys' room.'

Katie raises her eyebrows and points round the back of the shop. I go up a little alley to find the door marked Toilet and this is where I leave the next few minutes to your imagination...

On second thoughts, stop imagining! Let's just skip to me coming out again and glancing along the alley.

There's another door further up and by my calculations it must lead to the workshop. Remembering my orders, 'YOU. MUST. GO. IN. THE. WORKSHOP', I start walking towards it.

CHAPTER 8

Liquidate!

Jamie B., dressed in stylish black army-combat gear, stakes out the nerve centre of enemy HQ. He has to find out how evil Mr Dad plans to take over the world.

At the reinforced concrete perimeter wall Jamie B. pulls out a tiny laser-beam light-drill from the heel of his shoe. He shines it on the wall for a mere two seconds, blows away a slight wisp of smoke and peers through the perfect peephole he has created.

On the other side is a hub of activity: flashing control panels, scurrying scientists and high-speed buggies. At the very centre is a giant nuclear missile. The sign below it reads:

> **TARGET – LONDON**
> **Seconds before blast off:**
> 30, 29, 28, 27, 26...

Next to the numbers are two buttons: one red, one green. The green one is lit up like a traffic light on go, go, go.

Jamie B. scales the perimeter wall, swift and sure as a spider. It's one hundred metres high, but he isn't a highly-trained superspy for nothing.

19,18,17...

At the top of the wall B. stands and presses his belt buckle, unspooling meters of bungee cord. He fixes one end to the concrete with a tiny, barbed hook then snaps his buckle shut and prepares to jump.

If all goes to plan he'll dive down, press the stop button and be on the rebound before anyone even notices. He looks at the sign; it's now or never!

10,9,8,7...

Ready, steady, jump!

Faster than a Scud missile, Jamie B. swoops down and smashes his fist onto the red button...

5,4,3,2...

The clock stops - and so does Jamie B.

No rebound.

Someone must have cut the cable. He looks up to find hundreds of lethal laser guns pointing directly at him.

For a few moments time itself stands still—

Actually, nobody ever tells you how boring spying is. I must have been here an hour now and nothing's happened. Or maybe it has and I dozed off.

I'm hiding behind a pile of tyres and this is what I can see: men in protective masks; cars everywhere; sparks from a blow torch; the glow of a soldering iron here; someone removing a bumper there. Not exactly rocket science, is it?

In films, people always want to sneeze when they're hiding. Well I don't, but I do need the big boys'…sorry, men's room, again – badly. I'm just wondering whether to make a run for it when I hear voices.

'Is the Mercedes ready yet, son?' There's no mistaking that voice. It's as subtle as a sledgehammer – Mr Dad himself.

'No, Dad, all them other cars come in so we left it.'

'You what? We've got a special client for that Merc. What did you go and leave it for?'

'It's like you always told us, Dad, "Rule number one – when the old cars come in, drop the rest and get them sorted: doors, floors or bumpers, hide the…er, free gift there and ship them out pronto." In case of a raid.'

'You dip-stick! That Merc is 'otter than a sunny day in the Sahara! The accident showed up some of the old paintwork. I want it resprayed and off the premises sharpish. It's for my cousin's son so make sure you do a good job. He puts a lot of business our way.'

So, Stirling Leech is distantly related to Mr Dad. That I should have guessed – there's a striking similarity in the neck department.

And at least one of these cars is stolen and Leech's father is probably involved too. If that Merc is hot, I bet those cars coming in for repair are dodgy, too – but how? Is it something to do with those 'free gifts'?

I've actually got proof of Mr Dad's criminal

activity at last. Or I would have if my mini voice-recorder wasn't still at home under the bed in a box marked:

> SPYING: ALL THE THINGS
> YOU'LL EVER NEED – AND MORE.

I just didn't think I'd need them today, that's all!

After another fifteen minutes my bladder decides that I must make a run for the door – now! There's no time to hesitate, everyone seems busy so I make a dash for it. I've just got my fingers on the door handle when...

Whump!

It feels like an iron hand in steel gloves has just gripped my shoulder, 'Not so fast, boy!'

I'm wheeled around against my will and come eyeball to eyeball with Mr Dad. He's bending right over me and by the look of the purple blotches on his neck, he is not a happy man.

'You, boy, what did I tell you?' I feel his hot breath on my face like a blowtorch.

'D-don't. go. in. the. w-workshop?'

A second iron hand grips my other shoulder, sending needles of pain down my back.

'And what do you call this place?'

Good question. I could go for humour – 'Dog kennel?' – or ignorance – 'Dunno!' – but his grip is squeezing the words out of me like I'm a tube of truthpaste.

'Workshop.'

He relaxes his grip slightly, which is a relief as I think I'm about to pass out with the pain.

'How long you been 'ere?'

His eyes bulge fiercely and I do what any well-trained and honourable spy would do in my position – lie.

'Just came in. I finished washing the cars and wanted the b...bathroom. Katie said it was up here...'

Mr Dad clicks his fingers and one of the workers comes running.

'Dad?' (How many children has Albert got? Maybe he's planning to take over the world with baby Dads and Dadesses.)

'Phone through to Kitty. Ask if the kid just finished work. Tell 'er it's for the time sheets.'

Is this another code? Does 'time sheets' mean my time is up? Katie will tell him I finished nearly two hours ago and Mr Dad will decide to liquidate the only witness to his criminal activities.

Liquidate! or **Pulverise!** or *Terrorise!* or...

I see his son through the office window. He's got the phone in his hand, he's nodding. He puts the phone down and opens the office door, he's coming over...

TERMINATE! or **Disappear!** or ASSASSINATE! or...

'He's telling the truth, Dad. She says he finished washing the cars and asked for the bathroom a minute ago.'

Mr Dad lets me go.

Relief floods through me.

Literally. I've just wet my pants.

CHAPTER 9
The Honey Trap!

I think the spreading stain on my jeans is what really convinces Mr Dad I'm telling the truth.

'Go,' he growls, 'and don't come back.'

Sounds like a good idea to me.

Jamie B. unzips his overalls to reveal his snazzy designer skate gear in bullet proof silk. He unfolds a micro-skateboard from his pocket and leaps onto it.

Whoossshhhh!

But glancing over his shoulder, Jamie B. is stunned to see Mr Dad already screaming towards him on a super-adapted motor scooter, with Captain Bumsniffer clinging on behind.

The scooter headlights drop down and a gun barrel points in B.'s direction.

Pow!

Is this the end for our hero?

Jamie B. swerves to one side, out of the bullet's path, and ollies onto the kerb. Ahead of him is a flight of steps. He kickflips onto the handrail and grinds along it, sparks flying.

'Grab 'im!' shouts Mr Dad as the scooter bumps down the steps in hot pursuit.

Just as Captain Bumsniffer reaches out Superspy B. stamps down hard on the back of his board and lifts off in a jet-propelled rocket blast.

'Can't stop now - must fly!' Jamie B. calls out to the tiny figures below. 'Oh and watch out for the—'

Crash!

Jamie B.'s voice is drowned out by the sound of breaking glass.

Oops, didn't mean to skate over next door's bottles, left out in their driveway for recycling!

Skateboards rule though! Lucky I had mine in my backpack, along with some old skate clothes. So, I'm home and dry – literally – after some expert moves. Jamie B., of HMSS (*Her Majesty's Skateboard Service*), is back in control.

After a quick shower I cool down with an iced apple and mango cocktail (s. and not s.). Then I lie back on my bed and review the situation.

The facts

1. Mr Dad deals in stolen cars e.g. Stirling's Merc. This is illegal.

2. He hinted that his cousin, Stirling's dad, is involved in some way.

3. Mr Dad puts a 'free gift' in scrappy old cars which he sells for cash in hand.

Questions

1. Why did Katie cover up for me and what does she know about the plot?

2. Cash in hand means no evidence. How can I go to the police without evidence?

3. What's the 'free gift'?

*

You might think I can just turn up at a police station, tell them the story and let them go and find the stolen cars for themselves. Then they'd arrest Mr Dad and his cronies. Mission accomplished.

Well, it's not that easy.

I get up and look in the mirror. I see a suave, handsome superspy with ruthless eyes and a determined jaw.

The police might see a troublesome kid who's wasting their time. Don't ask me why but sometimes I think my undercover disguise is just too good.

What about Katie? Is she a double agent? She covered up for me but would she help me blow open the stolen car story and shop her own dad? Hard to believe. Anyway, how will I get to see her again now I've been fired?

My brain is as knotted as an assassin's garrotte. There's only one thing to do. Jamie B. rolls over and goes to sleep.

'Jamie, open up! There's a young woman to see you!'

M. starts hammering on the door again.

'What time is it?' I call, eventually struggling to the door.

'Six o'clock. I've just got back from work. What's happening, Jamie? What does that girl want?'

'Which girl?'

'The one from the garage. The one who nearly got you killed…'

I switch the decoder to Mute, leaving M. gulping like a goldfish, and go downstairs.

Katie is standing on the doorstep looking serious.

'I heard you got fired,' she says.

'Yeah.'

'Can I ask why?'

Suddenly I realise that M. is standing halfway down the stairs listening. I step outside and close the door.

There's not much room on the doorstep. I find it hard to breathe. Katie is just a kiss away. Don't get distracted, I tell myself. Remember the rules – mission first, romance later.

'I took a short cut through the workshop. It seemed to upset your dad.'

Katie gives me an odd look. She fixes me with those greeny-blue eyes – I'm drowning…

'We have to talk,' she says decisively. 'Can I come in?'

I remember the look on M.'s face when I closed the door and shake my head. 'Not here.'

She nods. 'Tomorrow then. I finish work early. Let's meet at the Snack Shack in town – half past three.'

'Sure.'

It's only as her footsteps click away down the street that a thought hits my brain like a poison pellet.

What if it's a trap?

CHAPTER 10

Mind Games

I stand in front of the mirror and lay out my weapons. Hair gel – check. Comb – check. Super-sporty, superspy body spray – check. Mouthwash – check.

I run through the drill in one minute, fifty-five seconds.

Splurge! Swish! Spray! Spit!

Fast, very fast.

I'm wearing black jeans, a black top and a large, black, super-modified wristwatch. Katie doesn't stand a chance.

Funny, really. I've been on dangerous missions before, of course, but this is the first time I've felt so nervous. My mouth is as dry as an extra dry Martini and I know it's because of the girl.

'Stay cool,' I tell my reflection. 'Superspies never get distracted by the love interest until after the action is over. Remember, the fate of the world – or at least local car drivers – is in your hands.'

So when I approach the Snack Shack and look in the window, I ignore Katie's wave. Instead I scan the place for enemy agents. By the time I've spied through the sixth window Katie looks totally fed up, but it's a price worth paying. Now I know the place is safe as a dead man's secret.

When I finally go in she smiles at me again, but I still have to finish my routine. I brush past her, heading for the toilet. Once there I test the window to see if it will open. Yes! And it's big enough for a super-fit superspy to squeeze through – the perfect escape route in case of emergencies.

Safety check completed I join Katie for my Coke, prepared in the usual way. 'Hi,' I say smoothly, and wiggle an eyebrow at her irresistibly.

She shakes her head. 'You are seriously weird.'

'Sorry?'

'All this checking out the windows and the

toilet – and checking out the workshop when you were told not to go in there. What is it with you?'

I shrug and say nothing. The important thing is to let her do the talking, find out what she knows. If she is a double agent she might let something slip.

She stares at me.

I stare back.

She stares harder.

The clock ticks.

I stare back.

The ice in my drink cracks. But I won't.

She stares even harder. Her eyes are stormy like thunderballs.

I keep my nerve and stare back some more.

Suddenly I see lightning flash and her eyes glow with anger. She stands up and slams some coins on the table.

'That's for the coffee – thanks for sparing me the time. See you,' she hisses.

She's picking up her jacket and I'm wondering if this is part of her plan. Can I really trust her?

'Wait.'

Her eyes flash again. 'Why? I thought you were going to tell me what's going on. What you saw in the workshop. Why you lost your job. Not play stupid mind games.'

That hurts. Games? International espionage is serious business, but she seems to have no idea. Poor innocent fool. So why did she lie for me? Can I tell her what I saw at the garage and trust her to keep it a secret?

'If I talk, will you go straight to your dad?'

'My dad? What's he got to do with…?'

Then she laughs and her eyes are as clear as the blue sky after a summer storm.

She sits down. 'My dad! You called him that the other day. You mean Albert, don't you?'

I nod.

'Albert is not my dad!' She pauses and looks at me through her long, dark eyelashes. 'I mean, do I look like him?'

'Well, not exactly…' Suddenly it's getting very hot in here. I take a gulp of my drink and nearly choke on an ice cube.

'It's because I call him Dad, isn't it?' she says, ignoring my spluttering.

'Th…that m…might have s…something to do with it!' I'm struggling for breath and she pats my back – hard.

'But everyone calls him Dad!'

'They do?' My eyes are watering now and she hands me a tissue.

'Didn't you notice?'

'I did think he had rather a lot of children.'

'He tells everyone to call him Dad. It used to be a family business when all his sons worked for him. Now they own garages in other towns but people still call him Dad anyway.'

'I don't.'

'Yes, well, I don't think you brought out his fatherly feelings.'

'Let's start again,' I say. 'More coffee?'

'OK, but let's hope you've actually got something to say for yourself this time.'

'They've got stolen cars in that workshop,' I blurt out, hoping I haven't shocked her too much.

'I know.'

'You know?' I say, totally shocked.

She nods. 'It's not just stolen cars…' There's

fear in her eyes now. 'Jamie, can I trust you?'

'Course you can.'

'I don't know, maybe it's best to keep quiet. Maybe I'm wrong…'

'You're not!' I say. 'Stirling's new Merc is definitely hot and Albert's cousin is involved too. I'm sure of it.'

'Yes, but it's something bigger than one or two stolen cars,' she says. 'Much bigger…'

CHAPTER 11

Include me out?

'Drugs,' she says.

'Drugs?' My head spins. Of course I know what they are. In fact I can't get away from them – lectures from M., visits from the *Dr No Theatre Company*, health classes at school – but that's just talk, or role play, or filling in the tick boxes on a 'Drugs Awareness Worksheet'. This is real life.

'Drugs?' I repeat stupidly. I swallow – it's like gulping down a cyanide pill. 'How do you know?'

'Albert was careless. That paperwork he left me. There was an extra sheet I've never seen before – a list of drugs, their names, weight and value, marked off against the cars. I couldn't believe it. He's always been so good to me.'

'I heard him say that every car had a "free gift". When the cars go in for "repair", they must hide drugs in the bodywork.'

Katie groans. 'He told me the cars were used for spare parts that were hard to get hold of. He said that's why people paid such a lot for them. I can't believe I was so stupid!'

'So who buys the cars?'

'Those cars are sent to Leech garages up and down the country, I suppose along with the so-called free gifts. They must have a network of buyers.'

I want to disappear into the toilets and dive out of the window right now. Jamie B. doesn't do drugs. Jamie B. doesn't want to know about drugs. Attempts to rule the world or break the bank of Monte Carlo he can cope with, but stolen cars and now drugs?

Mr Dad really is a villain. I can't slam the book shut or yell, 'Cut! Stop the film!' This is really happening.

Suddenly Katie's eyes widen. 'I can see Stirling outside!' she hisses.

'How much does he know?'

'Dunno, but I don't want him to see us together, he might suspect something.'

In an instant I'm slithering towards the toilets like a snake through sand. I keep my head low so I won't be seen from outside.

I close the door just in time but it doesn't keep out the sound of Stirling's voice.

'Ah, Kitty – what a pleasant surprise,' he booms. 'Looking forward to Saturday night?'

I hear a pitiful sound – like a trapped cat – and take it that Katie said yes.

'Well, I'll buy you a coffee to celebrate. Won't be a tick, just need to point Percy at the porcelain.'

I don't need a decoder to know that means he's coming my way.

My training pays off. My reflexes are on autopilot as I leap onto the sink and launch myself through the open window. Then I hear the door click just as I land in...well, I'll spare you the details, but let's just say this dog's owner has never heard of a pooper scooper. Of course, it's the extra icky-sticky type that won't ever come off your trainers.

I crouch down low and hold my breath. Only when the window is slammed shut and I'm sure

Stirling's gone can I breathe easy.

Well no, I can't breathe easy at all and have to hold my nose the whole way home.

I'm walking up our street when my mobile rings.

'It's me. I just got rid of Stirling,' Katie's voice whispers in my ear, making me tingle all over.

'Jamie? Hello?'

I pull myself together and try to act natural. 'Yes. I can hear you. How did you get my number?'

'You had to fill in contact details when you started work, remember?' Her voice sounds impatient. 'Listen, Jamie. Don't tell anyone what I told you. There's big money involved and it could get dangerous.'

'You have my word.'

'The question is, what are we going to do about it?'

It's a very hot day, but my hands are suddenly clammy and my spine turns into an icicle. I'm not scared, of course. Too many ice cubes in my coke, that's all. Still, I can't help thinking how easy it would be to say:

'Nothing.' OR

'Forget about it.' OR

'Include me out.'

Then I could return to HQ, detox my trainers and life would go back to normal.

On the other hand Katie said 'We,' and even though she's seventeen, she's asking my advice. Me, Jamie B., Superspy Extraordinaire – all my dreams of danger and action are coming true! It's time to live up to my name...but what if I mess up?

'Jamie, are you still there?'

'Uh-huh.'

'Well, are you in?'

I hesitate and take a deep breath. Yeuch – dog poo!

'Jamie? Are you going to help me do something about the Leeches' drug scam or not?'

'Yes,' I whisper. I'm holding my nose again but the sick feeling doesn't go away.

'Good. Now we need to come up with a really good plan.'

CHAPTER 12

In Too Deep

Jamie B., Superspy, sharply dressed in a black tuxedo, crouches under a table like a panther ready to spring. Only a white linen tablecloth lies between him and his evil enemy.

Jamie B. is no fool; he's prepared for a fight if discovered. He pats his inside breast pocket where his trusty .25 Beretta gun nestles next to his heart—

Stop! Time to kill the voiceover. I've got to get real. This is not the big screen. It's true life and it's happening now – there'll be no out-takes, no 'bloopers', no second chances. Think reality TV, Jamie. No...think reality.

Let me explain.

Yes, I'm crouched under a table – a table booked for the villainous Leech family.

Yes, I'm wearing a black tuxedo, and looking

quite sharp, admittedly. (Even M. said so, as she paid the hire fee…and put an embarrassing Cinderella clause in the contract, so I have to be back before midnight.)

No, I'm not carrying a gun – unfortunately. My only weapon is my hand-held voice recorder. But I hope that the evidence it gathers will be just as lethal in my quest for justice.

How did I get here? Don't ask. Yet another scramble through a toilet window – and it was the *Ladies*, too! The things I do for my country.

I'm at Swanks. Katie drove me here, flashed her ticket at the bouncer, then let me in round the back and hid me under this table.

She's driven off to collect Stirling now. The scary news is that both Stirling's dad and Albert are coming tonight. It's the presentation of the Inter-Schools' Rugby Cup: our school won, so the Captain of the Bumsniffers will be up on stage to collect it.

Stirling's dad – Mr Drummond Leech – is the guest of honour. He's some kind of businessman and Katie tells me they've just made him Town

Mayor as well.

At this point a solid, size twelve, black shoe kicks me up the backside and an unmistakable voice booms:

'Oh, sorry, Drum.'

Then an identical pair of solid, size twelve, black shoes deposits itself by my knees and says:

'What's that, our Albert?'

Don't look under the table, don't look under the table, I'm screaming silently to myself when a pair of leopard-skin kitten heels sits down and Katie purrs:

'Don't worry, Dad, I think you kicked a wooden leg, not a real one. No harm done. These tables are smaller than they look, aren't they?'

Phew! Katie's quick thinking stopped Albert rummaging under the table and blowing my cover.

Another pair of shoes joins them – too shiny and with fake gold buckles – and a horrible, hairy hand reaches under the table and pats Katie's knee.

'Playing footsie already, Kitty?' the voice says in an ear-splitting whisper. 'Save that for later.'

Katie's foot lashes out and I just manage to avoid her kitten heel as it digs into Stirling's shin.

'Oops, sorry!' she chirrups sweetly, but Stirling is howling like a wounded wolf.

'SHHHhhhh!' the Leech cousins hiss in stereo at Stirling.

'But—'

'That's enough.' Drummond Leech's voice is deeper and a bit posher than Albert's. He's definitely in charge at this table.

'This is a big night for the Leech family,' he says, 'and we don't want anything to spoil it.'

Suddenly a crash of thunder explodes above my head and I guess he's thumped the table.

'Do we all understand?'

'Yes, Dad.'

'Course we do, Drum.'

'Yes, Mr Leech,' Katie joins in – all sweet-voiced and innocent.

'Now here's Mother – looking·as beautiful as the day I married her.' A pair of strappy, red sandals moves in next to his.

'Let's drink a toast,' he says. There's a pause while everyone must be filling their glasses. 'To the family.'

'*To the family!*'

Chink!

'To business,' adds Albert.

'*To business!*'

Chink!

'To Stirling,' adds Strappy Red Sandals. 'Eighteen and a man today.'

'*To Stirling!*'

Chink!

'And tonight, my son,' Stirling's dad says, 'you'll enter the family business. One day you'll take over from me. What could be better? Keep it in the family. You can't trust anyone else...no offence, Kitty.'

'None taken, Mr Leech.' Kitty's voice sounds calm, but she crosses her legs and her foot is twitching nervously.

'Oh, Kitty 'ere is one of us,' Albert says.

'Worked for me, man and boy, since she was a kid. 'Aven't you, luv?'

'Yes, Albert.'

'What's with the Albert, all of a sudden?'

'Yes, Dad,' Katie whispers.

'That's better. You've called me Dad since you was about twelve and washing cars for us. Little tomboy then, but look at you now!'

I remember Katie when she drove up to collect me – with her curtain of red hair hanging loose and her shiny black dress showing curves in all the right places. It's suddenly very hot under the table. 'Play your cards right with our Stirling and you really could be family one day...' Albert stage-whispers.

Katie's foot is twitching even faster now – like a cat's tail when it's cornered.

Even though I'm hot and cramped under here with my tape recorder, I wouldn't swap places with Katie for a zillion dollars. If the Leeches find out that she is planning to destroy their cosy 'family business' they'll tear her to pieces.

Of course, she'd have me to defend her. But that's still two of us against three of them...four if you count Mrs Leech. And from the size of those strappy, red sandals, she's no push-over, either!

CHAPTER 13
The Truth

'And now, to present our Inter-Schools Rugby Cup we have a well-known local businessman and our new Town Mayor – Mr Drummond Leech.'

Everyone's clapping and I see a pair of size twelves disappear from under the table.

'Mr Leech will be presenting the cup to the winning team captain who, by a happy coincidence, is his son – Stirling Leech, eighteen years old today!'

More cheers, a quick round of *Happy Birthday to You* and Stirling's shiny shoes disappear as well.

More speeches follow, but I'm not listening. My foot has gone to sleep and this spying mission has turned out to be yet another disappointment. No one has said anything worth recording. The highlight of tonight was diving through the toilet window. Big wow.

'Ladies and gentlemen, it's a beautiful evening, so we've arranged for music and drinks outside in the gardens. Perhaps the Leech family will lead us out...'

The rest of the shoes disappear from around me but I hear Katie mutter something about powdering her nose. Then her bag drops on the floor beside me, and her upside-down face appears under the table.

'I give up,' I say.

'Jamie, you can't. We're in too deep.'

I knew she'd say that.

'No, we're not. I'm out – that's my last word.'

'But— Hang on. There's someone coming.'

Her face disappears for a while. Then there's a note passed under the table. It says:

Jamie,
The room is nearly empty. Give it five minutes, then meet me in the garden, behind the hedge on the left. Please.
Katie

It's written in lipstick with a mouth imprint by her name. Yes! She definitely likes me. OK, I'm young, but I'm very mature for my age and she's bound to have noticed. Perhaps I'll give her and the mission another chance.

It's dark under here. I light up my supersonic watch face, count five minutes, then scramble out from my linen cave.

The lights in the room have been dimmed and, through the French windows, I can see that it's getting darker outside, too. It's nearly ten o'clock and there are a few lanterns flickering in the trees but otherwise it's quiet and shadowy – just right for spying.

I head towards the music and laughter, threading my way through the trees on the edges of the garden, until I find the hedge and slip behind it.

Katie is standing in the shadows with two drinks in her hands. She looks so glamorous that, for a second, I'm speechless.

'Coke,' she says. 'Shaken, not stirred.' She hands me a glass and then lifts her own.

'To truth,' she says. 'Cheers.'

'Truth,' I echo and drink it down in one.

Katie looks at me hard. 'Jamie, I know you want out, but you heard what Drummond Leech said. They're going to introduce Stirling into the family business tonight. And we know what that means.'

'Surprised he doesn't know already. He must be really thick not to have noticed anything suspicious.'

'Well he's not exactly top of the class. Besides, I've known them for years too, remember, and I still find it hard to believe they've got this drugs racket going, even after discovering all the things we have.'

'OK, that's true, but what's it got to do with us, really?'

'Nothing, because we're not dumb enough to do drugs. Neither are they – but they're making money out of people who do. They're supplying dealers up and down the country.'

'So why should we be the ones to try to stop them? It's not our problem. I think we should just pull the plug on this whole mission before it's too late.'

She shrugs, 'Fine. Forget it, then. Like you said – why should you care?'

I'm feeling sort of hot and uncomfortable now. I loosen my tie but it doesn't help.

'Well, why should you care, either?' I say. 'Let's walk away now, Katie. This could get nasty.'

'It already has,' she says, lowering her eyes. 'My brother stole my CD player last week.'

'Sorry?' I need another reality check. This feels like someone's fast-forwarded a film and I missed a bit.

'He stole my CD player,' her voice is low and slow, 'then sold it to pay for his drugs habit. I don't know him any more…it's taken over his life. My mum and dad…' She breaks off and looks away.

'Aah.' Now I can see what she sees – Stirling Leech, the next Mr Big, expanding his drugs business while more people, like her brother and whole family, become the victims of his greed.

'OK, you're right,' I say. 'We've got to stop them. Someone has to.'

Suddenly my lips are warm. I can't believe

it – she kissed me!

I'm tempted to say I've changed my mind, then change it back again to see if I get more of the same treatment, but it's too late.

'Here they come now,' she says. 'You know what you have to do.' And she disappears into the night.

CHAPTER 14

Disaster Strikes

Hi, this is a live voice recording of Jamie B. on Saturday 10th August, 21.45 hours, in the grounds of Swanks Hall. I'm lurking in the shadows behind a hedge ready to change the course of criminal history. I can see the Leech family approaching and will hold the recorder out as far as I can to catch every guilty word. Here goes...

'...inside the driver's front door?' *(That's Stirling's voice – sounding less than confident for a change.)*

'That's right, lad. It's got a false interior.' *(Albert's voice – deep, broad.)*

'Not lad, Albert. He's a man tonight and finding out about a man's business.' *(Drummond Leech takes charge as usual.)*

'Right, Drum, point taken. This..."free gift"

is yours, Stirling. Not for personal use, o' course – none of us touch the stuff – you sell it.'

'And listen, young man; I'm your father, but if you're ever stupid enough to do drugs – hard, soft or whatever – you'll be no son of mine. Think of yourself as a businessman. There's money to be made here, so we build up contacts and get the best price. We must stay in control and that means staying clean. Got it?'

'Yes, Dad.'

'The first rule of business – let the market decide. If people want to buy drugs it's their choice. We just help them do it.' *(Drummond.)*

'Yeah. Ha. Business is business. Buyin' and sellin', that's all it is.' *(Albert.)*

'So, how much do you think my, er, "free gift" is worth, Dad?'

'Let's see. We'll start you off with the soft stuff – you can sell it to your mates. At current street value you'd stand to make…'

I want to catch Drummond's words but he's starting to walk as he talks. I try to move along and, at the same time, lean into the hedge a bit. That's when disaster strikes.

One minute I'm hiding behind the hedge, the next minute the branches give way and I'm sprawling into a crowd of Leeches on the other side.

I just have time to look up at three angry faces on three thick necks before they bear down on me as if they're the rugby scrum and I'm the ball.

'Jamie, over here!'

I hurl the voice recorder, like a hand grenade, in the direction of Katie's voice – just as the three Leeches collapse on top of me, crushing a few crucial bones.

'Get the girl,' Drummond orders and they're up again, forgetting about me – except for Stirling who gives me a quick kick in the ribs. Then he's galloping after Katie, too.

I can see drinks trays flying and hear the startled shrieks of guests but all I want to do is double up in pain and forget about the world...

*

It's not that easy. Katie's words come back to me. *You know what you have to do.* I stagger to my feet, clutching my rib cage.

Somehow I manage to stumble back the way I came: along the hedge, through the French windows, past the ghostly white tables in the dim dining room and out into the car park.

I can hear shouts now and, in a sudden burst of energy, I half-run towards Stirling's Merc, pull out the car keys that Katie gave me and fumble open the door.

There are footsteps on the gravel behind me – are they friendly or not? There's no time to check. My superspy instincts are kicking back in. I scramble into the driving seat, ram the car keys into the ignition and start the engine.

Then I remember. This is reality. And in reality I can't drive...

Seconds later Katie crashes into the driver's seat, nearly crushing what's left of my ribs. I'm still scooting over as the car screeches away and she pulls the car door shut. Then we execute a tight turn in reverse, nearly smashing into the three Leeches. I feel their fists pounding on the roof before we zoom off through the gates, their shouts ringing through the air like bullets.

Katie revs the car up from fifty to sixty to seventy – we both know that we must put as much distance between us and them before they start to follow.

CHAPTER 15

William Wayfinder

Even at top speed the car purrs along like a leopard. Katie's got the lights on full beam and they slice through the dark country lanes like swords.

I keep my eyes on the rear-view mirror until – all too soon – two more lights blaze into view, almost blinding me.

'They're following us,' I report, trying to sound calm.

Katie groans. 'Already? It looks so different in the dark and Swanks is way out of town. I think I'm lost...'

In front of us on the dashboard I see a red button marked WAYFINDER. We've got nothing to lose, so I press it.

'GOOD EVENING. WILLIAM WAYFINDER AT YOUR SERVICE. WHERE WOULD YOU LIKE TO GO TONIGHT?' asks a computerised voice with an

American accent.

'What was that?' Katie yelps in surprise.

'Must be an extra gadget Stirling had fitted when his car was repaired,' I say, thinking fast. 'William, we'd like to go to the fun fair on May Day Green.'

'**AFFIRMATIVE**,' William replies.

'Are you mad!' Katie screeches as she swerves around a zig-zag bend. 'What about going to the police?'

'We'd never make it in time,' I say. 'They're catching up with us already. The fair's nearer and—'

'**TAKE A LEFT HERE**,' William commands but Katie seems to be on automatic pilot and races ahead.

'**I SAID, TAKE A LEFT HERE, GODDAMMIT!**'

'Temper, temper, Mr Wayfinder,' I say, as Katie takes the turn at the last minute, screeching round the bend on two wheels.

'**PLEASE SLOW DOWN. YOU ARE GOING REAL FAST. THIS CAR IS A LETHAL WEAPON**,' William warns.

'Oh shut up, Willy,' Katie snaps.

I check the car mirror. The headlights disappear for a moment but then they're back again and gaining on us.

'Step on it,' I say. 'We're nearly there.' A map has lit up on the dashboard. It shows our route with the car as a bright flashing light moving towards a red dot.

'YOU ARE REACHING YOUR DESTINATION,' William tells us. 'PLEASE SLOW DOWN, THERE MAY BE A GATE OR BARRIER.'

He's right. There is a barrier.

Luckily it's made of plastic tape strung between two fences which rip and break quite easily when Katie crashes into them.

'OUCH – THAT HURT!' says William. He's far too sensitive – he'd never make a superspy.

'Get ready to bail out,' Katie warns as we lurch around the car park, which feels more like the recently ploughed field that it is. William comments on each bump.

'OUCH – THAT HURT!'

'OUCH – THAT HURT!'

I see the Leeches' car crash into the field now. It's a four-wheel drive and skims easily towards us.

Katie slams the car to a halt at the edge of the fun fair and we jump out. Ahead of us are flashing lights, blaring music and the hot, strong smell of fried onions.

Behind us is William's voice, getting fainter now.

'OUCH – THAT HURT!'

'OUCH – THAT HURT!'

'OUCH – THAT HURT!'

That's exactly what we'll be saying if the Leeches catch up with us.

'Here, take the voice recorder. I don't have a pocket – catch!'

Katie throws it over as I reach out – and miss! This never happens in the movies.

I scramble around in the long grass, losing valuable seconds.

'Come on – come on!'

Katie's grabbing my hand as I pocket the recorder and we run.

CHAPTER 16
The Big Prize

Adrenalin is pumping through my veins so fast we seem to be flying. Within seconds we make it to the heart of the fairground.

'Slow down, act casual,' I mutter out of the corner of my mouth, giving Katie's hand a quick squeeze.

We mingle with the crowd and I risk a look over my shoulder, hoping we've lost the Leeches. No chance! Three red faces and three bull necks are charging straight at us. Time to change tactics.

'Split up and run!' I yell above the thumping disco music.

Then, making the ultimate sacrifice, I drop Katie's hand and watch as she darts off to the left. I assess the situation. Ahead are the bumper cars, behind are the Leeches. One more second and they'll be on top of me.

The cars are spinning, the music is throbbing. Suddenly I **leap!** grabbing onto the pole of a passing bumper car and waving to the three astonished Leech faces as I twirl out of their reach.

'Two, please,' says one of the boys in the car and hands me some coins. He thinks I'm collecting fares and there's no time to argue because Albert and Drummond Leech have each squeezed themselves into a bumper car and are heading this way.

I pocket the money and look around frantically - time to **leap!** again. My feet scrape onto the bumper of another car while I grab the pole to steady myself. Just my luck to get a pair of maniac drivers – two giggling girls who are determined to dodge about and bump into as many cars as they can.

Crash!

I hold on tight.

BASH!

My knuckles are white and I'm getting a headache. But my superspy sixth sense tells me to look round. Just in time I spot Drummond

Leech on my left and Albert on my right. They're both speeding towards me like heat-seeking missiles locked on a target!

There's no escape. I close my eyes and…

Crack!

My body jerks back like a whip lash and pain shoots up my spine like a rocket. Rubbing at my neck to make sure it's still there, I open my eyes slowly. I'm alive! In a flash I realise that the maniac girls must have reversed very sharply. In front of me is the glorious sight of Albert's and Drummond's cars crashing into each other.

SMASH!

'Thanks for the ride, ladies,' I shout, taking my chance to jump off and dodge back into the crowd. They don't hear me, they're seconds from their next target…

BASH!

I wince and turn away, suddenly catching a glimpse of Katie's red hair. And the bad news is that Stirling Leech is closing in on her…

I reach into my pocket, slam the bumper car coins down onto the stall in front of me and grab three metal rings. But instead of using them to ring a teddy bear or goldfish bowl, I'm after a bigger prize tonight.

Balancing a ring between my thumb and forefinger I imagine skimming flat stones across a lake 1, 2, 3!

Swish!

The ring swirls through the air like a chopper blade and smacks Stirling on the shoulder, slowing him down.

Swish! Swish!

I send the other two rings sweeping after the first. One strikes the base of his skull. He bellows like a wounded bull and falls flat on his face. Yeesss! The old pain-in-the-neck technique never fails!

Katie spins round and rushes over. 'Thanks, he nearly had me there!'

Suddenly people are standing back and giving me strange looks. They must have been watching my ring-throwing routine but they don't seem too impressed. Someone is helping Stirling to his feet.

'Now what?' Katie asks.

I look up at the huge circle of lights spinning

in the sky.

'Over there!' I point. 'Buy some time...plan our next move!'

Once again we run, not daring to look behind. I feel like I'm in one of those repetitive dreams where the Leeches will chase us for ever...

CHAPTER 17
Fighting Destiny

As we run towards the big wheel it slows down and stops, but we have a problem. There's a huge man built like a bodyguard taking the money and there's no way he's giving anyone a free ride.

OK, so no self-respecting superspy should let a girl pay, but at this point I lose all self respect.

'Got any cash?' I ask Katie weakly.

She searches in the coin purse strung around her neck and hands over the money. We slam into our seats, bang the metal bar down across our knees and...

Nothing.

'Go!' I yell, rattling the metal bar in frustration.

The man gives me a look and there's something about the size of his neck that makes me wonder if he's related to the Leech family.

'Got a problem, mate?' he says gruffly.

Over his shoulder I can see the three Leeches have regrouped and are heading our way.

Katie suddenly takes the man's hand.

'We are so impressed with the size of your wheel,' she purrs in a voice that nuzzles up to him. '*Pleease* let us go up to the top RIGHT NOW and enjoy the view for a few minutes. I'd be so *very* grateful...'

Her eyes are wide and unblinking and the man looks mesmerised. He backs away and flicks a switch, giving Katie a little ruffled wave with his fat fingertips.

The Leeches' feet are pounding towards us but it's too late – the wheel creaks slowly round and we're whisked up into the air, swinging in our bucket seats way above their heads.

Jamie B. gets out his mobile phone and punches a few numbers. Time to make an important call.

The wheel stops at the top and we sway gently in the breeze, suspended between the earth and the stars. For once, Jamie B. can't think of anything witty to say. I just want to enjoy these precious moments of peace.

Katie's hair is blowing in the wind, her eyes are shining and I can hear her breathing. Time stands still and I feel like some great film director in the sky has led me to this moment – the moment when I will kiss her.

I may not have kissed a girl before (at least not in real life) but I'm not nervous. You can't fight destiny.

Cue sax music once more.

I close my eyes and pucker up...

Suddenly the wheel creaks and I jerk forward, cracking my chin on Katie's shoulder. She doesn't even notice, she's leaning over the safety bar and pointing below.

'Look, Jamie, there's no escape. The Leeches are waiting by the wheel exit. Even if the police get here fast, it'll be too late!'

The three ugly Leech faces swim into view and she's right, it's already too late – too late for us. The wheel is slowly turning and a voice inside me is yelling, 'Cut! Missed your kissing cue! Next scene...'

I am so angry that I stand up, reach into my

pocket and pull out the voice recorder, holding it high in the air so they can see.

'Jamie, what are you—?' Katie asks, but I'm already shouting, 'You want it? Go and get it!'

My voice rings out into the night and I throw the voice recorder as far as I can – like it's a ticking bomb with only one second left on the timer.

It catches the light as it makes a graceful arc over the fun fair stalls, past the parked vans and lorries and dips into the dark fields beyond.

There's a roar from the Leeches who charge off in that direction as the wheel brings us back down to earth.

'That was our evidence!' says Katie.

'It's not the only evidence,' I say. 'Come on – back to the Merc.'

Even as we reach it, the blue lights of a police car are flashing towards us. It bumps to a halt and a policeman and woman get out.

'Over here!' I yell. 'We made the call. Katie, open the driver's door.'

She does so and then stands back as I kick the

inside of the door, over and over again until the false interior gives way.

The police switch on their torches and their powerful beams light up some strange packages which have fallen to the ground.

CHAPTER 18

Love Interest

Town Mayor in Drugs Scam

ANDY MOLE REPORTS

Smashed by Young Superspies

PLUCKY YOUNGSTERS, Katie Cat (*17yrs*) and James Bradshaw (*12yrs*), tipped off police about a local-based criminal drugs ring on Saturday night.

Shocked onlookers watched in horror as Drummond Leech (*52yrs*), Town Mayor, was arrested at May Day Green fun fair along with his cousin, Albert Leech (*50yrs*) and son, Stirling Leech (*18yrs*).

They are being held at Crown Street Police Station pending further investigation.

Old Bangers?

It is alleged that Drummond Leech masterminded the scam. Leech is a successful businessman with links to companies overseas.

He passed on cars from his *Old Bangers* scrap-metal yard to his cousin, Albert Leech, owner of *Albert's Autos*. But the worthless old cars were simply a convenient cover-up for a complex drug-dealing network.

Big-time Crime

'This was a major break-though in the fight against crime,' said D.I. Julie Banks. 'We found drugs hidden in the cars under floors, behind doors and in the roof areas. They were sold to dealers via the family's network of garages all around the country.'

'The Leeches were such a well-respected family,' commented Mrs Ravi Khan (Deputy Mayor). 'Everyone is shocked. It took real superspies to expose this terrible scandal.'

'We do not recommend youngsters taking the law into their own hands – it can be very dangerous,' D.I. Banks warned. 'However, this time it worked out well and they did a brilliant job.'

Teens speak out

'I wasn't scared once,' said James Bradshaw (who prefers to be known as Jamie B.). 'Except when Katie was driving!'

'It helps keep drugs off the streets so I'm very happy,' added Katie Cat.

So this is it – action over, time for the love interest.

It's been a week since I last saw Katie, after the press interviews and photos. I suppose she just wanted a bit of time to herself.

Perhaps she was grounded, too. It's so unfair! First M. awards me with a hug, then she keeps me at HQ for a week for failing to meet the midnight deadline. She wouldn't even take the fact that we'd smashed a major drugs ring into consideration.

But now it's time for the romantic date. What should it be? A candlelit dinner for two at a posh restaurant always seems to work! I phone Katie's number...

'Table for two, Sir?'

'Yes, I have one reserved. The name's B., Jamie B.'

'Ah yes, Mr B., your usual table. If you'll just step this way...'

Jamie B. feels a thrill of pride as Katie Cat puts her arm through his. She looks stunning in a slinky, silvery dress.

The waiter shows them to a table discreetly tucked away in a corner of the restaurant.

'Oh Jamie, look at those roses, the candles and... this bracelet - can I really keep it?'

Jamie B. raises an eyebrow. 'Why not? Diamonds are forever, after all.'

Katie flicks back her shining red hair, exposing pale, bare shoulders, and looks at Jamie with glistening eyes.

'Alone at last,' she says. 'All this time and I haven't had the chance to tell you how grateful—'

'Nonsense,' he cuts her short. 'All in a day's work for B., Jamie B.'

'No, really, what you did for me was beyond the call of duty. After dinner you must come back for coffee so that I can...' she lowers her eyelids... 'give you your thank you present.'

'Hello?... He-*llo*.' Katie's soft, seductive voice has suddenly changed. She sounds brisk and annoyed. 'Is this a crank call? Hel-*llo*.'

'Katie, it's me.'

'Who?'

'Me, you know, Jamie. Jamie B.'

'Jamie! Sorry, we've had so many calls today. It's great to hear from you – gives me a chance to spread the news.'

So far, so good. She's obviously been

waiting by the phone for my call.

'What news?'

'My dad's got the chance to work in Europe for a year and we're all going with him – even my brother. He's trying to kick the drugs habit so a change of scene will really help. Isn't it exciting?'

'Europe? But...when...? What about...? I mean...aren't we going to see each other again?'

'Oh, Jamie.' Her voice sounds softer now. 'We had a great adventure together but...well, we're leaving in a few days and there's so much to do.'

'Leaving? So that's it then? Mission completed, over and out.'

'Don't be like that, Jamie. You've been a good friend. You really helped me out. I'm very grateful for all the risks you took. You were so brave, especially for someone who's only—'

'Hey, it was no big deal, you know, all in a day's work for me.'

'Thanks Jamie. I'll e-mail you – promise.'

'Huh! From Russia with love,' I mutter.

'Sorry? Russia? We're going to France.'

'France? Well...I...I hope things work out for you, Katie. *Bon voyage.*'

'Bye, Jamie. *Au revoir.*'

There's a click like the sound of a trigger being pulled. I put down the phone and stagger backwards as if I've been shot.

CHAPTER 19

Fatal Wound

'Jamie…'

M.'s coming up the stairs but this is no time for a debriefing. I slip into my room and close the door.

There's a tear on my cheek, but don't tell anyone, will you? For your eyes only. After all, Jamie B. doesn't cry. That's not his style.

I lie on my bed and think. Mission completed. Bad guys behind bars. It's a happy ending, right? Then why do I feel so bad? There's a pain as if Katie's shot a fatal bullet right through my heart.

I've seen the films, I've read the books – the superspy always gets the girl…doesn't he?

M's knocking on the door now.

'Jamie, can I come in?'

I don't answer, which means no, but she comes in anyway – we seem to have a communication problem here.

I roll over and turn my face to the wall. She sits on the bed.

'Is everything OK?'

I don't want to talk but M. must be using some kind of truth dart. As soon as she puts her hand on my shoulder the pain gets worse and I'm muttering into my pillow:

'Katie...she's leaving. The whole family... France...a year.'

'Oh.'

I wait for the cheers and the official government health warning about her being too old for me, but it doesn't come.

'You really liked her, didn't you?'

I nod as best I can but nearly suffocate in the process. So I take my head out of the pillows and sit up.

'Well, I must admit that I do think you got involved with something way over your head...'

I get ready to switch on the decoder.

'But...'

I pause.

'I can understand why you liked Katie.'

This is worrying. Does Mum hear the sax music when Katie's around too?

'You know, Jamie. You and Katie were fighting for something important that you both believed in. I wish you hadn't taken so many risks but you acted very bravely. No wonder you feel close to Katie – you worked as a team.'

'Mmmm.' I'm trying to speak but my voice box is immobilised – I'm in bad shape.

'I owe you an apology, Jamie. I was still seeing you as my little boy, playing at spy games and living in a world of make-believe...'

It's definitely truth dart time – I bet that's how Katie sees me too. She doesn't know how much I grew up this summer – and that hurts!

'...but after this I have to get used to the idea that you're becoming a young man.'

'I am,' I say, or rather squeak. What's wrong with my voice? I clear my throat and try again. 'You're right, I am,' I say in deep, manly tones. 'You know sometimes, Mum, I think you know me just too well.'

She smiles. 'I'm proud of you, Jamie B.'

*

M. is holding an X-ray up to the light.

'Congratulations on another successful mission, Jamie B.'

'Thank you, M. I have discharged myself from the rest home and am reporting for orders.'

'Don't be ridiculous, look at this wound. The bullet nearly pierced the heart - it could have been fatal.'

'But as a superspy it is my duty—' Jamie B. starts to protest, but winces with pain and suddenly sits down.

'It is your duty to get better. An injured spy is no use to anyone. Now, take a holiday, Jamie B. That's an order!'

Yes. I think I will give spying a rest for a while, take some time out... I still need to cover expenses, though. Maybe I'll take M. up on her offer after all, and do a few hours in her salon. Undercover of course. I wouldn't want to be recognised.

As for the wound, I know it'll stop hurting sometime.

Then it'll be, Look out world – Jamie B. is back in action!

And you'll barely see the scar...

Orchard Red Apples

❏ **The Poltergoose**	*Michael Lawrence*	1 86039 836 7
❏ **The Killer Underpants**	*Michael Lawrence*	1 84121 713 1
❏ **The Toilet of Doom**	*Michael Lawrence*	1 84121 752 2
❏ **Maggot Pie**	*Michael Lawrence*	1 84121 756 5
❏ **The Snottle**	*Michael Lawrence*	1 84362 344 7
❏ **The Fire Within**	*Chris d'Lacey*	1 84121 533 3
❏ **IceFire**	*Chris d'Lacey*	1 84362 373 0
❏ **The Salt Pirates of Skegness**	*Chris d'Lacey*	1 84121 539 2
❏ **Do Not Read This Book**	*Pat Moon*	1 84121 435 3
❏ **Do Not Read Any Further**	*Pat Moon*	1 84121 456 6
❏ **How to Eat Fried Worms**	*Thomas Rockwell*	1 84362 2068
❏ **How to Get Fabulously Rich**	*Thomas Rockwell*	1 84362 207 6
❏ **How to Fight a Girl**	*Thomas Rockwell*	1 84362 208 4

All books priced at £4.99

Orchard Red Apples are available from all good bookshops,
or can be ordered direct from the publisher:
Orchard Books, PO BOX 29, Douglas IM99 1BQ
Credit card orders please telephone 01624 836000 or fax 01624 837033
or visit our Internet site: www.wattspub.co.uk
or e-mail: bookshop@enterprise.net for details.

To order please quote title, author and ISBN
and your full name and address.
Cheques and postal orders should be made payable to 'Bookpost plc.'
Postage and packing is FREE within the UK
(overseas customers should add £1.00 per book).

Prices and availability are subject to change.